LEGO CITY

LEGO® CITY EMERGENCY

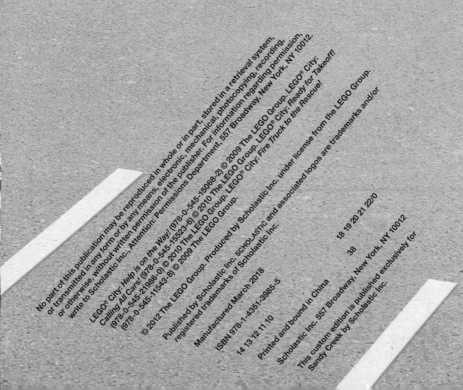

HELP IS ON THE WAY!

By Sonia Sander

Bear walks Jessie to school.
He barks at the cars as they cross.
Woof! Woof!
Beep! Beep!

Bear follows Jessie home, too.
But today, Bear is not there.
Uh-oh, where is Bear?

But he hasn't.
No one Jessie asks has seen Bear.
Oh, no, poor Bear is lost.

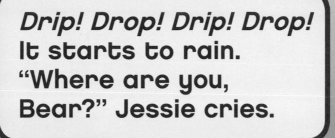

Drip! Drop! Drip! Drop!
It starts to rain.
"Where are you,
Bear?" Jessie cries.

Jessie hears Bear cry.
She finds him in the park.
Poor Bear is stuck under a gate!

Bear needs help fast.
Jessie asks the police for help.

The worker has a saw to cut the gate. Z-Z-Z-Z-Z-Z!

C-r-r-r-e-e-a-k-k!
Jessie's new friends lift
the gate off Bear.

The workers take good care of Bear.
They wrap up his paw.

28

Bear gives Jessie a big, wet kiss.
Jessie hugs Bear.
She says, "Now we can go home!"

LEGO CITY

CALLING ALL CARS!

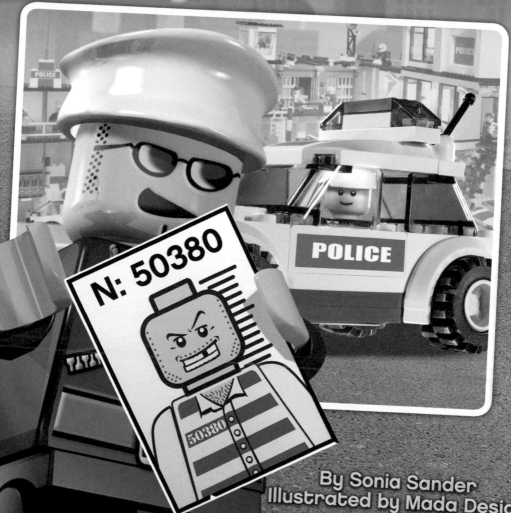

N: 50380

50380

POLICE

POLICE

By Sonia Sander
Illustrated by Mada Design

One! Two! Three!
Three crooks make a run for it.

They speed off in a van.
Z-o-o-o-m!

The police race to the bank.
Lights flash and sirens blare.

The police look for clues.
They watch the bank video.

Outside, the police ask questions.
They find out about the van.

The police study the clues.
Now they know who to look for.
They will look for a red van.

The crooks go to jail.
Slam!

LEGO® CITY

READY FOR TAKEOFF!

By Sonia Sander
Illustrated by Mada Design

GATES
A1-A3
←

GATES
B1-B3
↑

GATES
C1-C3
→

Where is the gate?

It is time to board.
Take out the plane ticket.

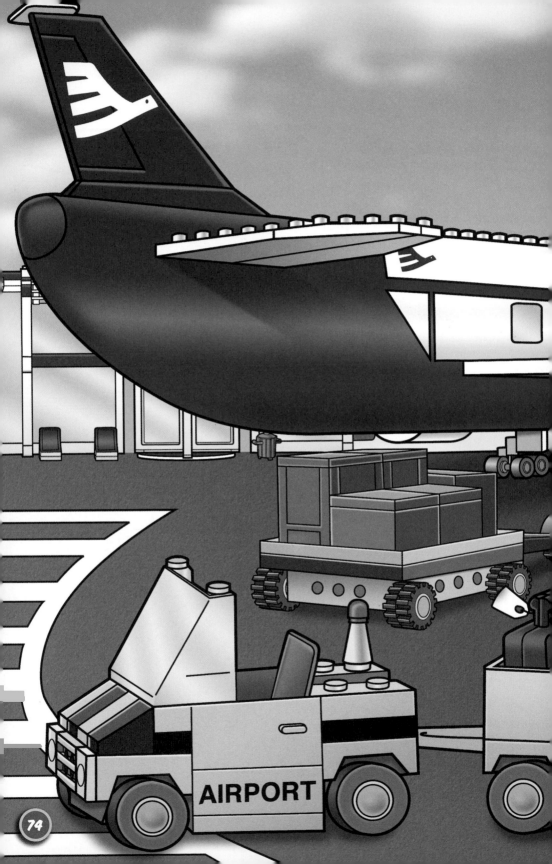

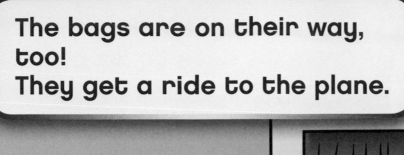

The bags are on their way, too!
They get a ride to the plane.

75

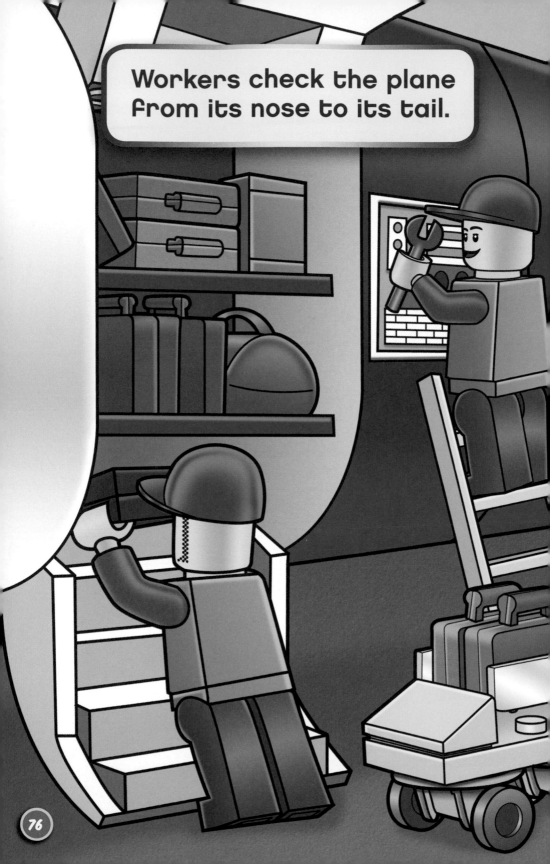

They fill the plane with gas.

The pilot is ready in the cockpit.
The ground crew shows the pilot where to go.

The planes wait their turn. The tower tells the plane when to take off.

81

It is time to fly!
The plane speeds down the runway.
V-r-r-r-o-o-o-m!

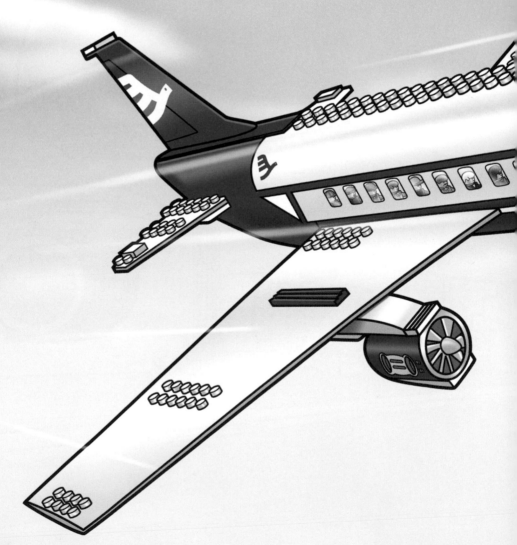

The plane flies into the sky.
It soars above the clouds.

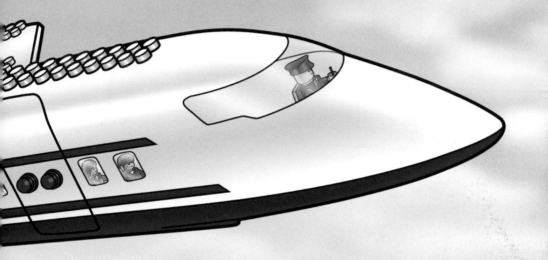

Look out the window.
See how small the city looks.

The plane flies a long way.
One last turn before landing.
Down come the wheels.

89

Bump! Bump! Whoosh!
The plane slows to a stop.

AIRPORT

Find all the bags!
One! Two! Three!

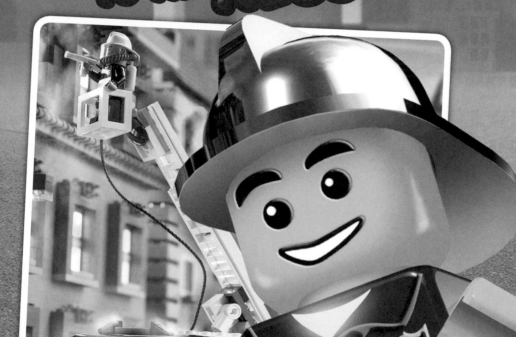

LEGO CITY

FIRE TRUCK TO THE RESCUE!

By Sonia Sander
Illustrated by MADA Design

Call 911 right away!
The firefighters can save the day.

B-r-r-r-i-i-i-n-g!
The fire alarm rings.
The firefighters are on their way.

102

One by one, they jump into action.
They slide down the pole.

The firefighters dress in a flash.
They grab their hats and boots.

W-o-o-o-o! Honk! Honk!
The fire truck races down the road.

There is no time to lose.
It is time to fight the fire!

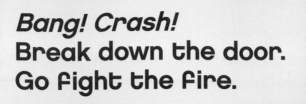

Bang! Crash!
Break down the door.
Go fight the fire.

Meow! Meow!
Up goes the ladder. One brave
firefighter saves the cat.

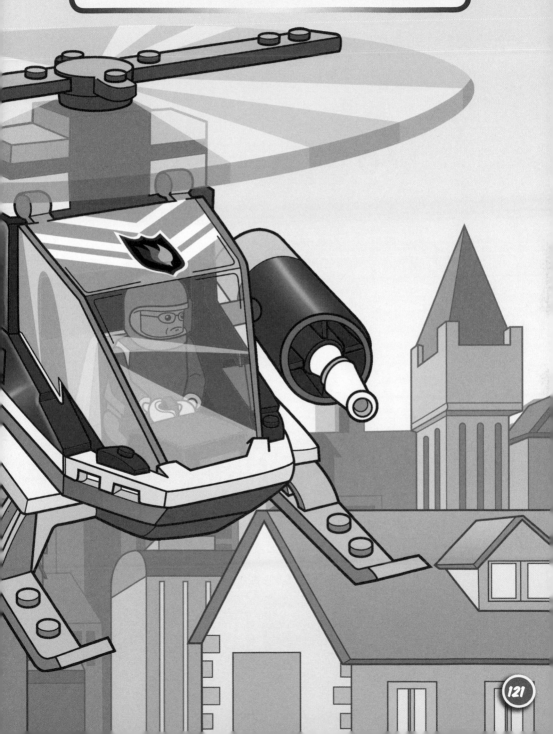

Look high up in the sky.
Here comes even more help.

Water sprays all over.
The fire starts to die down.

At last the fire is out.
The tired firefighters head home.

It has been a very long day.
The firehouse is quiet for now.
Only a few soft snores can be heard.